Tiny frogs,
giant toads.
Count them up,
loads and loads.

Frogs from Spain,
frogs from France.
Some can sing,
some can dance.

HOWAR... ...BOLDT

Tommy Fox
owns a box.
In the box?
Lots of frogs.

Rushing to
show-and-tell.
Just in time –
there's the bell.

Into school,
"ribbets" loud.
Classmates all
form a crowd.

Box jumps left,
box jumps right.
Tom holds on,
squeezes tight.

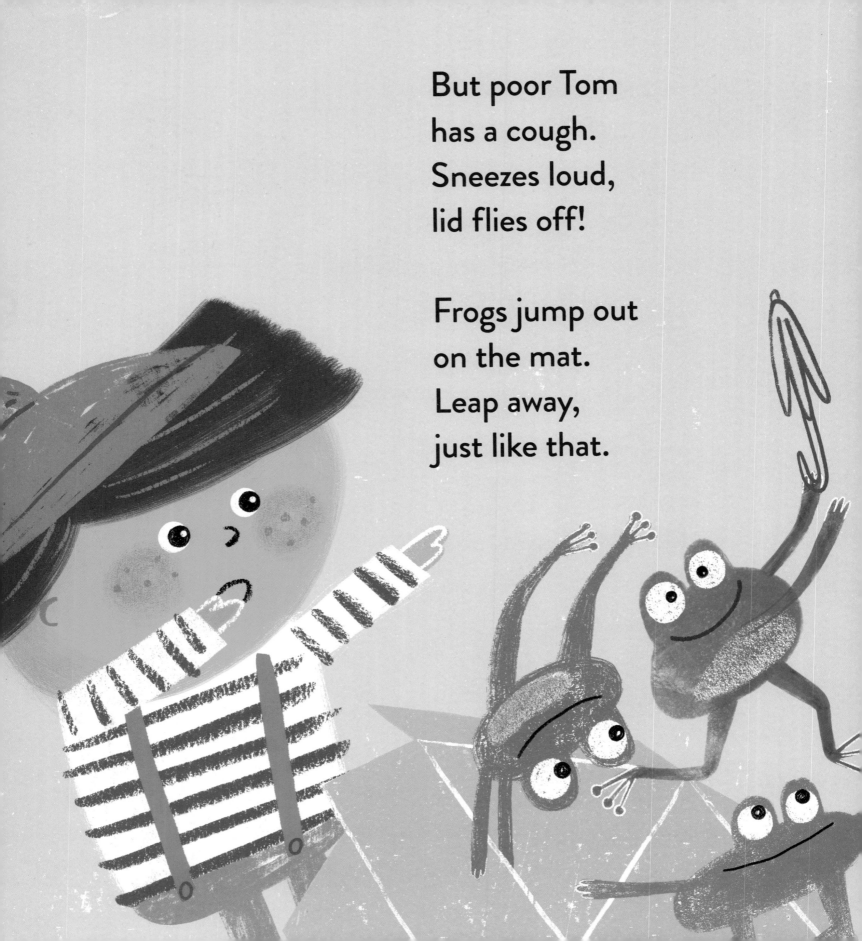

But poor Tom
has a cough.
Sneezes loud,
lid flies off!

Frogs jump out
on the mat.
Leap away,
just like that.

All the frogs
go berserk.
Screams and shouts –
no more work!

Children laugh,
teachers shriek
as frogs play
hide-and-seek.

Frogs in coats,
frogs in shoes.
Frogs in sinks,
more in loos.

Mr Fisher
tells them off.
Tongues stick out,
teacher's shocked.

Tom's not sure
what to do.
Bounce, bounce, bounce –
there's a clue!

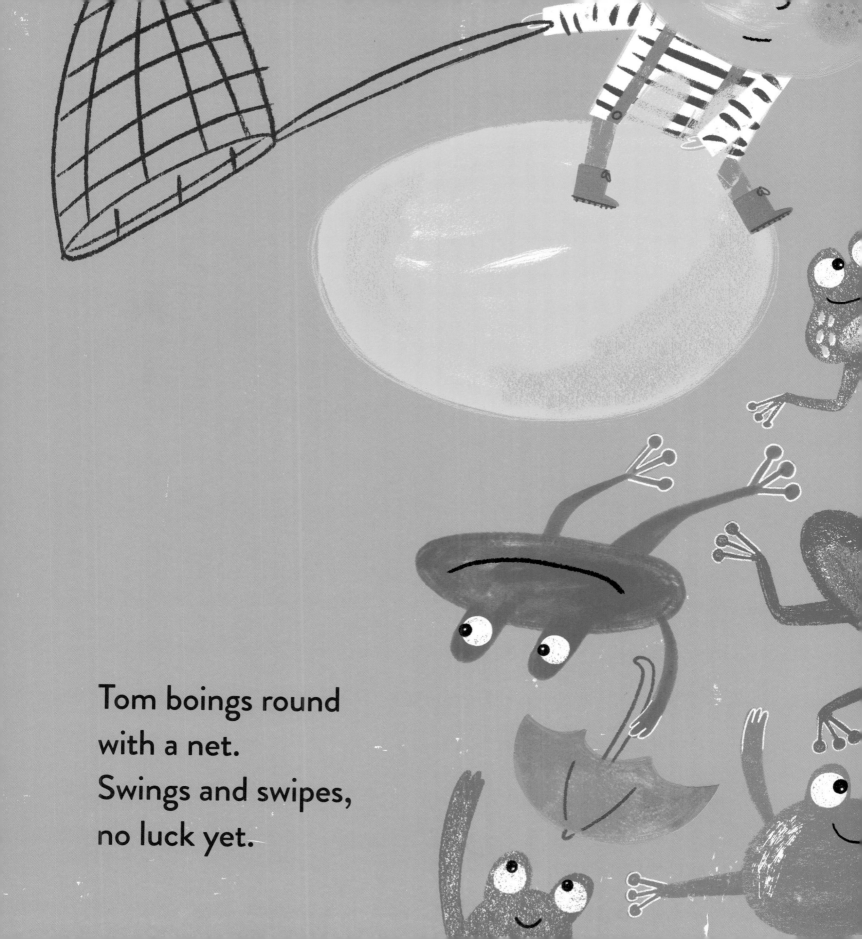

Tom boings round
with a net.
Swings and swipes,
no luck yet.

But he's quick,
bounces fast.
What's he caught?
A frog! At last!

One, two, three
in the net.
Four, five, six,
lots to get.

5

6

7

8

9

10

Frogs are in
hopping heaven.
Snatches one,
that makes seven.

On a roll,
eight, nine, ten.
Some spring out . . .
start again!

More, more, more,
in they go.
Round the school,
Tom's not slow.

Net's quite full,
halfway there.
Look! There's five
on teacher's chair!

Staffroom next,
do they dare?
Three jump in
Headteacher's hair!

Rows of frogs
drinking tea.

Catching bugs,
full of glee.

In the hall,
frogs steal food.
Croak and grunt,
how very rude!

Tom bounds in
while they eat.
Scoops them up
off their feet.

Now he's got
one to go.
Searches high,
searches low.

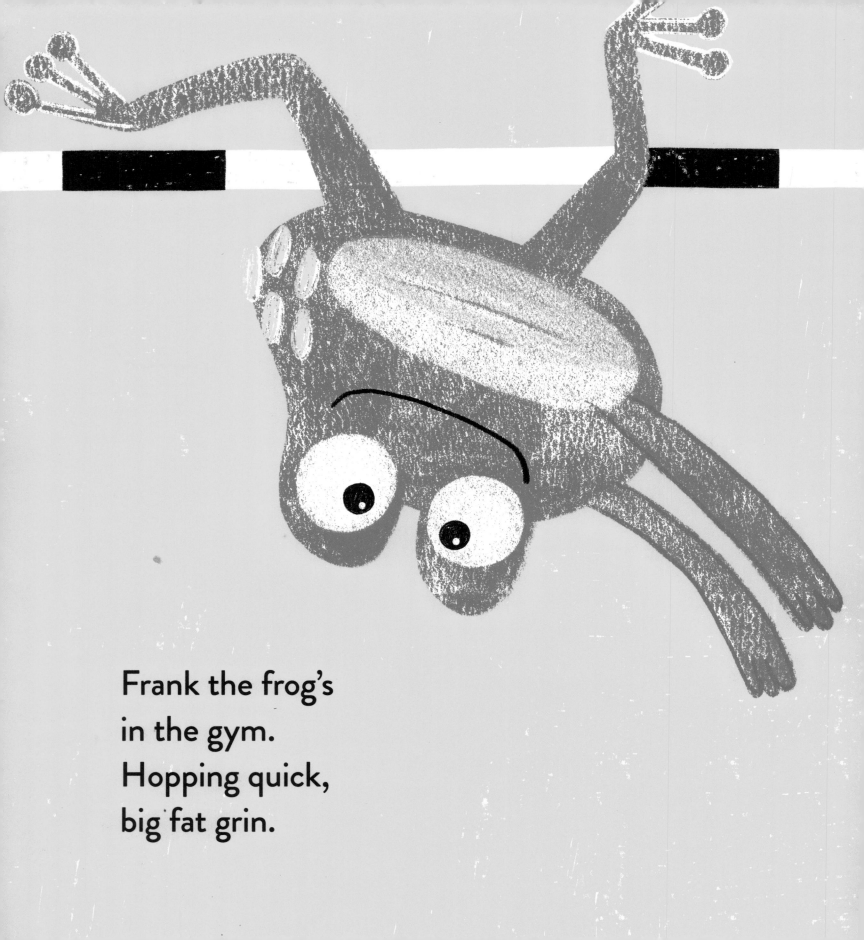

Frank the frog's
in the gym.
Hopping quick,
big fat grin.

Climbs up rope,
can't be stopped.
Waves at Tom
from the top.

Fly flies by,
Frank's tongue pops!
Falls off rope . . .

. . . lands in box!

All the frogs
in the box.
Tom smiles wide,
then he . . .